Angels at Bedtime

Angels at Bedtime

Tales of Love, Guidance and Support for You to Read with Your Child—to Comfort, Calm and Heal

WATKINS PUBLISHING

LONDON

Angels at Bedtime

Distributed in the USA and Canada by
Sterling Publishing Co., Inc.
Sixth Floor, Castle House, 386 Park Avenue
New York, NY 10016-8810

This edition first published in the UK and USA in 2011 by
Watkins Publishing, an imprint of Duncan Baird Publishers Ltd
Sixth Floor, Castle House, 75-76 Wells Street
London W1T 3 QH

Managing Editor: Sandra Rigby
Senior Editor: Fiona Robertson
Managing Designer: Suzanne Tuhrim
Commissioned artwork: Tina Mansuwan

ISBN: 978-1-78028-026-4

10 9 8 7 6 5 4 3 2 1

Typeset in Filosofia
Colour reproduction by Colourscan, Singapore
Printed in Singapore by Imago

For information about custom editions, special sales, premium and corporate purchases, please
contact Sterling Special Sales Department at 800-805-5489 or specialsales@sterlingpub.com.

A NOTE ON GENDER
In sections of this book intended for parents, to avoid burdening the reader repeatedly with
phrases such as "he or she", "he" and "she" are used alternately, topic by topic, to refer to your
child or children.

Contents

About This Book

"Relax, be very still and listen carefully to this story ..."

These words, which begin every tale in this collection, will transport your child into the magical world of the imagination, a world in which angels can be found just as easily in a shoebox or a playground puddle as flying up in the sky. It is the openness and innocence of children, and the power of their imagination, that make them so receptive to perceiving signs of the angels who constantly watch over and guide us all.

By reading these stories of the miraculous ways in which angels come to our assistance, you will help your child to see the magic that lies just below the surface of everyday life. And once you have sparked your child's imagination, there's no limit to where it can take him: by encouraging your child to identify with the characters and settings, and to talk about the illustrations, a single story can be the jumping-off point for many new adventures.

These stories about angels work on different levels. Each one is an exciting tale in its own right, set in either a modern-day environment that your child may well have experienced (such as a family holiday or a school playground) or in the fairy-tale world of princesses and giants that all children love. But each tale is also a parable of difficulty overcome, and many of these will have direct relevance for a child who may already have encountered sibling rivalry, peer pressure or the challenges of a new step-family.

The affirmations at the end of each tale draw out its essential messages – perhaps that bullies are bullies because they are frightened of something, or that people will respect you if you own up to your mistakes. And each story describes a different way in which angels intervene in our lives, so that story by story your child will build an understanding of how the angels work.

These tales about angels are perfect for bedtime reading. Each one will leave your child with the calming sense that, despite the very real difficulties we encounter in life, the world is an essentially benign and moral place. They have been written to appeal to children aged between four and eight, but this is only a suggested age group. You, as the parent, will know when it is time to read stories about angels to your child.

It's a good idea to read the introductory section before you start. Pages 9–12 explain all about angels and how and why they appear in our world. Pages 13–25 explore how storytelling can meet the needs of children. On pages 26–7 you will find a quick relaxation exercise to practise before the storytelling commences. This can help your child to shake off the cares of the day and prepare to enter the world of the story.

If you are looking for a tale to illustrate a specific value or problem, turn to the index on pages 141–4. Also at the back of the book (from page 134) is a section on visualization that explains why the skill of conjuring up mental pictures at will is useful to a child, and how you can teach it to him. Have a go at the fun guided visualizations. These will help your child to take the stories in this book further, to develop imaginary worlds and maybe even to meet a guardian angel of his own. The wonderful thing about angels is that the more we look for them, the more they appear in our lives.

Who Are the Angels?

The word "angel" means "messenger", from the Greek *angelos*. In cultures all over the world we find these mysterious and awe-inspiring beings who intercede between the world of the transcendent and the confusing, frustrating and sometimes frightening human world in which we are often in need of guidance and help.

In the Christian and Jewish Bibles and in the Koran, angels bear messages from God to humankind. The birth of Jesus Christ, to provide salvation for all mankind, was announced to Mary by the Angel Gabriel. The angels in these ancient sacred texts guide, protect and comfort just as we imagine angels doing today. You may have seen the beautiful painting "The Annunciation" by Leonardo da Vinci which shows a winged, human form with flowing locks, wearing long robes and featuring an expression of immense gentleness, grace and beauty, kneeling before the Virgin Mary. Some of these characteristics were used to describe angels in the Old Testament, while others have been elaborated and refined over centuries of Christian art.

Yet this is only one way in which angels have appeared in our world. Tribal societies would identify our "angels" as

9

the spirits that are linked to every person, in the same way as trees, mountains, rivers and indeed everything in the natural world have their own associated spirits. In Hinduism what we call angels are devas, benevolent spirits associated with moral values or aspects of nature, such as wind, fire and air. The angelic devas of the Theosophists are nature spirits who protect the natural world and actively intervene in human life.

Angels are neither male nor female, neither human nor divine. We don't really know what they look like. All we can know is how they choose to appear to us. The stories in this book are full of surprises: an angel might appear as an animal or an old lady, as a message in a puddle or a voice on a radio. It's as if angels know best how each person will recognize them and change their form accordingly.

Whether angels inhabit the heaven of the Christians, Jews or Muslims, or the stars and sun as the Theosophists believe, or a parallel dimension that is interwoven with, yet separate from, our own, all we can know for sure is that their love and guidance have helped innumerable people in need from the very earliest times all over the world.

How Angels Help Us

If you gather together at random a group of people and ask if anyone has ever been helped by an angel, there will always be a few who say, "Well, I can't say that it was definitely an angel, but there was this one time …". Perhaps you have your own recollection of a stranger who gave good advice just when it was needed, or of a comforting sensation that someone was watching over you during a dark period of your life. As this collection shows, angels don't necessarily appear to us as obviously supernatural beings and their actions are not necessarily miraculous.

Many people have sensed a strange presence close by when they were threatened by physical danger. During the perilous final stages of his ascent of Everest, after his climbing partner had been forced to turn back, the mountaineer Sir Francis Smythe became convinced that a friendly, protective being was climbing beside him. He wrote afterwards that he had no fear of falling, so sure was he that the being would catch him if he slipped.

Sometimes an angel will intervene directly to save a life, as in the story "The Proud Prince" (page 84), in which Prince Hector is saved from falling by an angel in the form of a tree. More often, however, it is the consciousness of an angel's presence that fills a character with confidence, as in "The Heroine of the Crow's Nest" (page 28), in which an angel helps Jaya to steady her nerves for a safe descent of the ship's rigging.

Angels can inspire us to undreamed-of success, but we have to be open to their message. It may not come from the direction we expect. In "The Nesting Swallows" (page 46), it is the sight of the birds building their marvellously intricate nests with great patience and effort that inspires Lin to take her piano-playing to new heights.

Sometimes an angel may help without appearing at all. The empty space of a box is enough to inspire Princess Iris with beautiful dreams of angels – and love for the gift's unknown donor, a lowly footman but the only man imaginative enough to deserve her ("The Little Wooden Box", page 36). In "The Smallest Giant" (page 74), it is merely the angelic sound of the little girl's voice that encourages the giant Tim to protect her. Angels work in subtle ways – we need to keep our eyes and ears open.

The Best Teaching Tool

Children (and grown-ups!) love stories, and for that reason a good story is the best way of communicating ideas of right and wrong. Children who put their hands over their ears when told what to do will listen eagerly if they are charmed with interesting characters and an exciting plot. They will remember the story and therefore the message long afterwards — just think how many of the stories that you loved as a child you still remember now. Jesus understood this, and the Buddha too: both used parables, or simple tales, to help people to absorb complex messages.

Childhood today is portrayed as being under siege from the materialism of the adult world as never before. We worry that our children will acquire a consumerist mind-set in which only branded possessions provide a basis for "cool", and that self-respect and old-fashioned values are too often forgotten. These stories about angels will nurture your child's sense of right and wrong, showing how values such as honesty ("The Honest Shepherd", page 94), loyalty ("Dad's Big Day", page 102), sharing ("The Old Man and the See-saw", page 66) and compassion ("The Smallest Giant", page 74) are more valuable than any possession.

Children will love these stories about angels because the human characters are no angels themselves. In "The Wisdom in the Puddle" (page 118), Jack is the bully's friend and it takes the intervention of an angel to help him to overcome his distrust of the strange, quiet Stevie and the peer pressure from his friends to exclude Stevie.

By showing how the angels care for us, all these stories illustrate the most important value of all: love. Angels only act in the best interests of those they help, gently guiding the characters to make the most of their lives. They watch over and help us, yet they ask for nothing in return.

Building on the Stories

As the parent or carer, you will be best able to judge when to discuss the underlying message of a story and when to let a story simply speak for itself. If you feel that your child needs help with a particular issue covered by one of the stories, you can encourage her to explore it in more depth by making up her own stories and drawing pictures, or perhaps by acting out a play using dolls or puppets or creating a game based on the story. Imaginative play like this will help your child to understand the message of the story, as well as nurturing her creativity and self-confidence.

Coping with the Real World

However much we want to shelter our children, we cannot prevent them from encountering difficult situations as they grow up. Nor, indeed, would we want to. It is by facing up to a bully or by overcoming shyness and reaching out to a new friend that children develop self-confidence and learn how to stand on their own two feet. But childhood is more complicated than it used to be: adult stress filters through to our children, who feel compelled to look right, own the right things, have the right friends. At the same time, a trend toward parental separation and remarriage turns many children's lives upside-down, with families broken up and new ones created. Childhood can be an unsettling and difficult time.

The stories about angels in this collection can help in three ways. Firstly, they acknowledge that problems such as shyness, jealousy or insecurity happen to children just like yours. They provide comfort to a child undergoing similar difficulties: he knows he is not alone.

Secondly, the tales provide practical advice for handling a variety of situations that your child may encounter in his own life or the lives of his friends: sibling rivalry ("The Old

Man and the See-saw", page 66), parents divorcing
("The Mysterious Cowboy", page 88), being bullied
("Odd One Out", page 108), jealousy of a new baby
("The Kind Monkey", page 114).

Finally, by telling your child stories about angels,
you are teaching him that someone is always looking
out for him as he confronts difficult periods in his life.
A child who knows to ask the angels for guidance will be
able to draw on their wisdom and love to see him through
the darkest times.

Time Out with Your Child

The frantic pace of today's world means that parents often feel guilty that they
don't spend enough time with their child. Yet, as "The Flying Horse" (see page
40) illustrates, a parent's loving attention is the most important thing in the
world to a child. Storytelling is a wonderful way of providing your child with
your complete, focused attention. It also gives your child an opportunity to
raise any related concerns about his own life – or perhaps remind him to
share a recent discovery or triumph with you. The more interest you show in
the kind of person that your child is becoming, the more you listen to his
fears, hopes and wishes, the happier and more confident he will be.

A Child's Imagination

Imagination is the key to a child reaching her full potential. Many specialists in education and child development, such as Friedrich Froebel, Rudolph Steiner and Maria Montessori, have stressed the importance of imaginative play in a child's earliest years, insisting that it far outweighs the value of traditional schooling in numeracy and literacy. In this play-centred approach, providing a child with a box of sensory "treasures", such as a pine cone, a scrap of velvet and a shiny spoon, or offering her a few old clothes to dress up in, or giving her a simple rag doll to cuddle, is much more valuable at this stage than trying to drill the ABC. Creative play has been shown to help the development of an impressive range of skills, from empathy and compassion to communication and problem-solving.

As a child plays, she practises living – how can she achieve her best if she has never imagined it? Yet the imaginative activities in which older children once revelled are no longer so freely available. Gone are the days when children would be encouraged to be out of the house in the morning and allowed to run free until supper time.

The risks are now considered too great and children are corralled in supervised activities or allowed to while away the hours in front of the television or games console, their creative faculties on hold. So the parents' role in stimulating their child's imagination is all the more important, whether that be through taking her to the seaside or a museum, talking to her about different cultures and different eras of history, or telling her as many stories as possible. Feed your child's imagination and watch her grow.

A child's imagination also provides a safe space in which she can learn about the different ways we relate to each other, as well as the difficult situations that she may well, one day or another, have to face in real life. She may already have encountered some of the challenges described in these tales about angels, but there will be many that she has not thought about before. Meeting them in a story told by a parent provides her with an opportunity to explore painful emotions, such as the fear of the death of a beloved relative ("Grandad's Pumpkin", page 32), before she has to deal with anything similar in the real world.

A child does not necessarily accept the story that is being read to her in the same way as she might do the pictures flashing on a television screen – completely and unquestioningly. Instead, she questions everything: Why did he do that …? What would happen if …? She retains control as she manipulates the plot as her imagination dictates, and enters and leaves the story world at will. Her ability to make a story her own means that it is an ideal tool to help her to resolve her conflicts to her own satisfaction.

The Miracle of Language

Every healthy child develops the ability to use our incredibly complex and subtle system of language simply by experiencing the speech of others. There is no need for any formal training for this to happen, but you can certainly nurture your child's interest in books and her delight in using words by reading to her from the earliest days. Babies are charmed by rhymes and words set to music, and they love looking at pictures and trying to point out the things they can see. The first word usually comes between twelve and eighteen months of age. Between the ages of four and seven language skills explode, as children start creating complex sentences and building up vocabulary. Now is the time for you to play around with rhymes, puns and word games, to tell stories and to encourage your child to read and write.

The Art of Storytelling

Bearing in mind the vital importance of developing a child's imagination, you may feel overawed at the responsibility of assuming the role of storyteller – and scared that your performance skills are not up to scratch! Don't be. Fortunately for those of us who are not actors or professional storytellers, a child's imagination is so powerful that firing it needs only enthusiasm and openness to the magical world of stories.

Enthusiasm really is important. If you are thinking about your day at the office or the chores still to be done, your tone will convey your disinterest and undermine the experience for your child. If you, as storyteller, are not interested, how can you expect him to be? Make up different voices for the characters and don't worry about sounding silly. Use your voice and facial expressions to convey your awe when the angels reveal their presence. Throw yourself into the tale and you might find you are as swept away by the wonder of it all as your child.

The key rule of public speaking also applies here: go slowly. Speak clearly and introduce pauses for dramatic effect or when you can see your child is pondering something. If he is keen to ask you a question in the middle of the story, don't insist on making him wait until the end. Answer his question and then carry on. Make sure you allow plenty of time for the whole experience.

If he's not dropping off to sleep when you've finished, you could encourage him to share his reactions to what he's heard. It can be tricky to strike a balance between drawing out his ideas and not making him think you are testing him. Try to avoid talking too much about your own thoughts at the expense of your child's response. If he starts talking about something apparently unrelated, give him a little time. It may be bedtime, but perhaps he is working up to sharing a concern that the story has provoked.

Each story is accompanied by a colourful illustration. Ask him about it and see where his imagination takes him. He'll love identifying the characters and the settings, and perhaps he'll tell you why one of the characters looks different in his imagination. What can he see in the background? A detail like a little bird or a winding path might set him off on a whole new imaginative adventure.

Letting Go of the Day

Children often find it hard to concentrate at the best of times and this is particularly so at the end of the day, when they are tired and may be fretful. These stories about angels are a lovely way for your child to disengage from the troubles and excitements of the day, and prepare for sleep. Surely there can be no more pleasant way of drifting off to sleep than soothed and inspired by a wonderful tale of angelic love and guidance.

You will probably need to prepare your child for the bedtime story so that she's in a receptive frame of mind. Child-care experts suggest that it's a good idea to use the same bedtime routine at the same time every day – for example, supper followed by a bath followed by a story (not necessarily about angels). A familiar routine helps your child to relax and leads her step by step toward sleep. During this time, it's best to use a calm, quiet tone of voice and avoid subjects that are likely to cause arguments. Before you start reading, try a quick relaxation exercise (see pages 26–7) to release any excess energy.

If you want to keep these stories about angels special, try telling them only at a certain time and on certain days.

Bedtime is the ideal opportunity, but if that
is not suitable you can pick some other occasion;
maybe when your child has finished homework
or after supper. If your child knows when to
expect an angel story – perhaps on a Sunday
night, signalling a new week – the anticipation
will heighten the experience and enhance that
particular night with a sense of ceremony.

Using Visualization

One way of plunging your child into the world of the story is through
visualization (see pages 134–40), by asking her to conjure up a mental picture
of the scene she is about to enter. Before you begin telling the story, try
encouraging your child to imagine what she can perceive with all her senses.
For example, in "The Heroine of the Crow's Nest" (page 28), you could
encourage your child to see herself standing on the dock beside Randolph
as the millionaire's great ship makes ready to set sail. What can she smell?
Fish, perhaps, and the tar on the ship's hull. What can she hear? Sails
snapping, the rigging jangling in the wind, the shouts of the crew. What can
she taste? Sea salt and the apple she's brought in her pocket. What can she
feel? The oily railings that she's gripping, the buffeting of the wind. And
what can she see …? That's a whole new story.

Using Affirmations

These stories about angels are essentially joyful: their message is that the real world in which your child lives is a magical and loving place in which angels can appear at any moment, if he only looks for them. Of course the characters in the stories face problems with friends, family and teachers just as he does, but the tales teach that following certain codes of behaviour will, like the cloud of fireflies in "Light in the Dark" (page 70), ultimately lead us through the blackest of caves. This outlook, that we can change our lives for the better by changing our behaviour, is a positive one that many adults are guilty of forgetting. But if we ourselves do not face the future optimistically, how can we expect our children to do so — however much we may want this?

At the end of each story are three affirmations that will help you to draw out its positive meaning for your child. One affirmation often describes the truth about angels that the story embodies, perhaps that angels help us to find the strength that we didn't know we had, or that angels want us to see the best in other people. The other two affirmations draw out the values that the story embodies, whether that's the advice that things are a lot less scary if you face your fear ("Lost in the Wood", page 124), or that putting yourself in someone else's shoes will help you make up a quarrel ("Odd One Out", page 113). To avoid sounding like a teacher or talking down to your child, ask him what he thinks of the affirmations as though you'd really value his help in working it out together. Children love feeling that their ideas are important and useful.

Helping Children to Be Confident

Children need to value themselves if they are to have the confidence to experiment and grow to their full potential, but self-praise is not something that happens naturally. We all (children as much as adults) have a certain idea of ourselves and our strengths and weaknesses, and it is all too easy for a child to become dismissive of his own abilities, whether in the schoolroom or the playground. A child needs your help to learn to value himself. Don't let him tell himself that he's "rubbish at that". Instead, spend a few minutes before your child goes to sleep going over the day's successes – there will always be something of which he can be proud. Helping Mum with the washing up and behaving well at bathtime can be as praiseworthy as three gold stars from his teacher or a sporting victory. A child who acquires the habit of valuing himself will grow up trying his best.

Let's Begin

Even after all your efforts to create a calming bedtime routine, your child is probably still going to have the fidgets when it comes to story time. To help her to relax and let go of all the excitement and frustrations of the day, try this quick and easy relaxation exercise. It's a simple technique that will help your child to shake off pent-up energy, leaving her calm in body and mind and ready to concentrate. If your child enjoys it, you could incorporate it into every bedtime. As the stretching routine becomes second nature to her, she will be able to draw on it whenever she feels unable to sleep.

Ask your child to lie on her back on her bed (or on the floor with a pillow or cushion supporting her head), with her legs and arms straight and her hands comfortably by her side. Then in a quiet, calm voice say to her:

"Close your eyes and listen to your breathing. You are breathing gently in … and out … In … and out … In … and out … Now take in a deeper breath … and as you blow it out, imagine you are blowing out all the butterflies in your tummy. Now slowly take in a really big breath and imagine you are filling up your whole body with air like a balloon … Now slowly let the breath back out … As it goes, you are sinking back down onto the bed (or floor).

Now imagine you are squeezing an orange in each hand. Squeeze as hard as you can. Squeeze out every last drop of that orange juice. Feel how strong and tight your arms and hands are, then let go. Relax. Let all the tension go. Feel how loose and floppy your arms and hands are now.

Now stretch out your legs as hard as you can. Point your toes forward and then backward. Point them forward, then backward. Forward, then backward. Now relax your legs and toes. Feel how loose and floppy they are now.

Now squeeze the oranges in your hands, stretch your legs and point your toes again, and at the same time scrunch up your face into the smallest ball you can make. Squeeze up your whole body. Now relax. You are sinking back onto the bed (or floor). Your whole body is loose and floppy and there's a lovely warm feeling moving up from your toes, to your knees, to your tummy, to your elbows, to your neck, to your head. Now you are ready for the story. Let's begin."

The Heroine
of the Crow's Nest

Relax, be very still and listen carefully to this story about a girl called Jaya. She worked for a rich man, Randolph Rosher, who lived in a mansion by the sea. Jaya spent most days cleaning, scouring and scrubbing. But one special day Jaya did something very brave indeed.

It was a bright, breezy day in summer. Final preparations were being made for Randolph's wedding to his beautiful bride, Rose. Randolph was down in the harbour inspecting his magnificent sailing ship. It was to take him and his new wife on their honeymoon after the ceremony. The ship had been washed, painted and polished until it gleamed. Lines of colourful bunting fluttered in the breeze and there was even a red carpet set out, awaiting the arrival of the bride.

Randolph was very pleased as he took in all the preparations. But then his face darkened with anger.

"What's the matter with the flag?" he shouted, pointing to the top of the mast. The new flag had been designed with

Rose and Randolph's initials embroidered together in a beautiful knot. But it was a very windy day. The flag had become tangled just above the highest part of the ship's mast — at a look-out point called the crow's nest. All the crew pulled and tugged at the rigging, but the flag would not budge.

"There's only one thing for it," said Randolph. "Someone must climb up the rigging and free the flag."

One by one the sailors gave excuses why they couldn't possibly do it. "I have a bad leg," said one. "I get dizzy," said another. No one had volunteered when tiny Jaya shyly pushed to the front of the group.

"I'll climb up," she said to Randolph, "I don't mind heights too much. I'll try to free the flag."

The other workers started sniggering. "Who does this nobody think she is?" muttered one of them.

Without another word Jaya started to climb. Up, up, up she went, until finally she reached the crow's nest. A crowd had gathered to watch and there were gasps as the little girl tugged at the flag, balancing on the very edge of the crow's nest high above. Finally, the wedding flag flew free.

As Jaya started back down, the wind blew harder and the ship began to rock. Far below, waves crashed against the ship's hull. Suddenly her foot slipped from the rigging! She was paralyzed with fear as she clung to the ropes.

Just then, she heard a soft and soothing voice. "You won't fall, Jaya," the voice said. "You can do it. Believe in yourself." Jaya became calm and unafraid. She couldn't see who was speaking, but she sensed a presence close by. She recovered her balance and climbed steadily down the swaying rigging.

When she reached the deck, the crowd broke out into a chorus of cheers. As he congratulated and thanked her, Randolph told Jaya of the miracle that they had all seen. As she slipped and clung to the rigging, an angel appeared fluttering below her, holding out a magical net like a butterfly collector's net. The net had been there all along to catch her if she fell.

Affirmations

- Angels watch over us all the time and are there to help us whenever we are in danger.
- Believe in yourself and you will be amazed at how you are able to achieve extraordinary things.
- Everyone has their own special talent, even if the people around them haven't noticed it yet.

Grandad's Pumpkin

Relax, be very still and listen carefully to this story about a girl called Emily, who is helped by angels in a most extraordinary way. Close your eyes and imagine you are lying in a beautiful garden. You can feel the sun warm on your face. It is so lovely and peaceful that you can hear a bee creeping into a flower and a ladybird crawling up a stem.

Now, Emily's grandad was a gardener and one day he gave her a special pumpkin plant. "It needs sunshine and shelter from the wind," he said. "And always give it lots of water." Emily thanked him. She was very excited and promised to look after the plant.

But the very next day, Grandad had to go to hospital. When Emily's mother went to visit, the doctors told her that he was ill and must rest for a long time.

That summer it was very hot and it hardly rained at all. Soon the lakes and reservoirs began to get low. One morning,

33

Emily's mother came into the garden. "We're not allowed to use the hose to water the garden any more," she said. "There isn't enough water to go around."

"But my pumpkin will die!" cried Emily. "I'm growing it specially for Grandad so he gets better."

Emily's mother sighed. It seemed to Emily that Mum always looked sad these days. "Sometimes miracles happen," Mum said. "Grandad used to tell me that angels were always watching over us."

"Even in the garden?" asked Emily.

"He said they were everywhere," replied her mother.

Emily sat down in the shade of an apple tree. She spent most of her time in the garden when she wasn't at school and she'd never spotted an angel anywhere. She shook the hosepipe to see if there was a drip left for her pumpkin. There was nothing.

The days went by and there wasn't a cloud in the sky. Everything in the garden began to dry up and wither.

One afternoon, Emily sat down by her pumpkin plant. The leaves were turning yellow and the little pumpkin underneath was beginning to shrink. She knew it would die without water. Emily put her hands over her eyes and wished for a miracle with all her might. If Grandad was right and there really were angels everywhere, surely one would help her now.

That moment, a cool shadow passed over her and Emily felt her skin tingle. She looked up and saw a small grey cloud floating above her. Fat drops of rain began to splatter on the ground!

From then on, Grandad started to get better and a little rain fell on the garden each day. By the end of the summer, Grandad was well again and the pumpkin was huge and round and orange.

Emily knew that Grandad had been right all along. Angels do watch over us everywhere.

Affirmations

- Looking after a special gift shows how much you care about someone.
- Never give up when something seems hopeless – if you are patient it often turns out right in the end.
- The power of love and positive thinking can make miracles happen.

The Little Wooden Box

Relax, be very still and listen carefully to this story about a princess called Iris and a very special wooden box — a box that filled her heart with angel dreams. Close your eyes and imagine the beautiful palace where Princess Iris lived.

Now this princess was very popular — she was kind and funny and clever. All the princes in the neighbouring lands wanted to marry her. So one day her father set a challenge.

"Whoever brings a present that can keep Princess Iris happy for a year, may marry her," King Julius said. "He will be the man best suited to my daughter."

Soon, the great hall in the castle was piled high with gifts. But the princess was not allowed to know who they were from — that would have been cheating. Among the presents were 365 boxes of chocolates (one for each day of the year), a golden mirror, a canary in a cage, a silver flute, the rarest orchid in the world and buckets and buckets of jewels. There was also a small wooden box with nothing in it.

Princess Iris was soon sick of chocolate. She had no interest in mirrors or jewels. She felt sorry for the canary and set it free. She didn't know how to play the flute and the orchid made her sneeze. Only one present intrigued Iris — the little wooden box.

She carried it with her everywhere, peering into it. Sometimes she smiled. Sometimes she laughed. Sometimes she was sad.

"Whatever does she see in that thing?" wondered King Julius. "It's empty!"

Carl, one of the footmen, was standing close by on duty. He knew what she saw. But he said nothing.

"Obviously, the box is from a rich prince," declared the Lord Chancellor. "If Iris agrees to marry him, it will always be filled with gold."

"Beware! It is the gift of an evil enchanter," warned the Royal Doctor. "The box will steal her breath away."

"It must be from a trickster!" giggled the Jester. "The box will explode with a horrid eggy smell!"

Still Carl said nothing.

When the year was up, King Julius called for the man who had given the box. "You may claim my daughter's hand," he said. Nobody noticed Carl step forward — except Iris herself.

"Go on!" she whispered.

But Carl was afraid to speak up. He was just a servant. Then Iris smiled and he felt brave. She looked as beautiful as an angel, full of joy and love.

Carl cleared his throat and bowed to the King. "It was I who gave the wooden box."

"You?!" said the King. "Why such an odd present?"

"I had no money for a fancy gift," explained Carl. "But, because the box was empty, I hoped that Princess Iris could imagine it full of anything she wanted."

"I imagined it filled with dreams of angels," smiled Iris. "Dreams of adventure ... of longing ... of hope ...." She took Carl's hand and kissed it. "And also of love!"

And so the footman and the princess were married.

I imagine they were very happy. Don't you?

Affirmations

- Angels can help us to discover how imagination makes even the most ordinary things exciting.
- Sometimes the simplest gifts can be the best.
- We need to find the courage to follow our heart and show our feelings, even when we are afraid.

The Flying
Horse

Relax, be very still and listen carefully to this story about a nobleman's daughter called Marina, who made a very special angel friend.

Marina was spoiled. She only had to ask for something and it was hers. She was the finest rider in the land and she had a stable full of horses and all the grooms and stable hands she needed. She could jump higher and gallop faster than anyone else. But Marina also had a big problem. She was always angry. No matter how patient and kind other people were, Marina snapped and shouted at them.

Some people said that Marina was born under a bad star. But the truth was that Marina was angry because she was unhappy and lonely. She had no one to talk to. She lived on her own with her father, Lord Vincent, in their big house and he was always away on the king's business.

Lord Vincent had made her a promise: they would spend her twelfth birthday

together. The day arrived and, excited, Marina
rushed downstairs to have breakfast with him.

But her father wasn't there.

"Don't be angry," said Nellie, her old nursery maid,
when she saw Marina's face. "Your father works hard for
the king so that you can have whatever you want."

"But I don't want lots of things," shouted Marina,
smashing her bowl on the floor. "I just want Father to be
here. He promised."

"He's only following orders. He has to do what he thinks
is best," said Nellie. But Nellie really thought that Lord
Vincent should have tried to be with his daughter on
her birthday.

Marina slammed the big front door and stomped off
down to the stables to see her horses. She rang the bell
to call her grooms, but there was no reply. Then she saw
an old man leading a magnificent white horse down the
path toward her.

"Who are you?" demanded
Marina rudely.

"A messenger," said the old
man. "I have brought you a present
from your father."

"Why couldn't he bring it himself?" shouted Marina. Then she looked at the beautiful horse and something made her change inside. Instead of feeling angry, she wanted to burst into tears.

The horse stepped forward and bent down on one leg. Without a word, Marina climbed onto his back. When she looked down, the old man had disappeared.

Later, people said they had never seen a horse gallop so fast. They saw it jump over hedges so high it seemed as if it were flying. All the while Marina clung to the horse's mane and the anger and loneliness she had known for so long blew away like the wind in her hair.

Time flew by and when Marina turned to go home, she felt happy and her heart was as light as a feather. And she knew it was because at last she had found a friend.

As Marina slid down the horse's neck, she thanked him for the day they had spent together. She wondered where on earth her father could have found such a wonderful creature.

"I shall call you Pax, which means peace," she whispered in his ear. She led Pax to a clean stable and gave him lots of oats and water.

Marina was bursting to tell someone about the strange old man and the mysterious horse. She ran back to the house as fast as her legs could carry her. When she walked through the front door, she could hardly believe her eyes. Her father was waiting in the hall, with all his luggage!

Marina ran straight into her father's arms. They hugged each other for a very long time without speaking.

"Marina, I am so sorry," said Lord Vincent eventually, taking his daughter's hand and looking at her very seriously. "I should have spent your birthday with you as I had promised. And because I was in such a hurry to come back, for the first time ever I have no present to give you."

"But you sent me the beautiful horse," said Marina. "And he's my dearest friend in the world."

Lord Vincent smiled at her happy face but he had no idea what she was talking about. "What horse, dearest?"

"The one the old man brought me," said Marina. "He said it was a present from you."

Lord Vincent shook his head in amazement. The strange thing was, the previous night Lord Vincent had dreamed about an old man leading a magnificent white horse. The old man had warned him not to break his promise to his daughter. He said she needed Lord Vincent's love and attention more than anything else in the world. The next morning Lord Vincent hadn't been able to forget the dream. He believed the old man was an angel, so he had left court and spent all day travelling back to his daughter. And now they were together.

"I don't care about presents," said Marina happily. "Come and meet my beautiful new friend." But when they got to the stables, the horse had gone!

"Oh, where is he?" cried Marina.

"Don't worry," said Lord Vincent, and he told her about his dream. "Angels come to help us but they don't spend long on earth."

Marina smiled. "So long as we are together, nothing else matters," she said.

Affirmations

- Sometimes we need the help of an angel to understand our true feelings and know what is the right thing to do.
- When a person is very angry it can mean that they are upset and unhappy and need our kindness.
- Love is the greatest gift we can give to anyone.

The Nesting
Swallows

Relax, be very still and listen carefully to this story about a little girl called Lin. She wanted more than anything else in the world to do well in a piano competition. The music Lin was practising sounded like it should be simple to play, but she was finding it very hard until some little feathered angels helped her.

Lin's parents were poor farmers who lived in a tiny village in the middle of China. Her father, Geng, raised pigs for market and her mother, Mei, embroidered quilts. One day, when Lin was four years old, a travelling musician visited the village. His name was Yi and he played a piano on the back of his wagon.

Lin watched entranced as Yi played for the village. After he had finished she climbed onto the wagon and, to everyone's amazement, began to play.

"Your daughter is a musical genius," said Yi to Lin's father. "She must be taught by a professional."

"But we have no money," said Geng. "How can we afford to buy her an instrument or pay for her teacher?"

Yi loved music and he could not bear the thought of Lin's great talent going to waste. "I will sell you my piano for almost nothing," he said, "so that your daughter may learn to play."

Lin's parents gratefully accepted Yi's offer. Her father gave Yi his savings and her mother gave him her most beautiful quilt. In return Yi carted the piano to the farmhouse and promised to send them a music teacher when he reached the next town.

Lin learned quickly and soon people came from all over the province to hear her play. They loved her music so much that they gave gifts of money, which meant that Geng and Mei could carry on paying for Lin's teacher.

Years passed and then, one day, Lin's teacher told her about a piano competition in a nearby city.

"The winner will get a scholarship to the Academy and a prize of ten thousand yuan!" he said. He pointed his finger at her. "Lin, you must win this prize. It is your duty to your parents."

"I will do my best," replied Lin.

"You must do more than your best," said her teacher,

giving her a sheaf of music. "The most talented pianists from all over the country will enter this competition. The other students might be better than you."

It was spring and all the trees and hedges were covered in blossom. Birds sang in the sunshine, and bees and insects buzzed among the flowers. Lin and her teacher sat together at the piano on the veranda and she listened as he played the music. It was unlike anything Lin had ever heard. At first the music sounded simple. Then, as her teacher played, the notes of the piano changed. They were like the sound of a stream splashing over rocks or the gladness in your heart when spring turns to summer.

Afterwards, Lin tried to play the sheet music she had been given. Because it had sounded simple she thought it would be easy. But this was the most difficult piece of music she had ever tried to play in her life.

"Don't worry," said her teacher. "Practise hard and in time you will be able to play it well."

A month went by. Lin's piano teacher listened to her play and sat with his head in his hands. "Oh dear," he sighed. "You sound as if you are playing with your elbows."

Lin shook her head. "This music is too difficult for me," she said.

"Everything worth doing is difficult," said her teacher. "Look around you. You'll find a way to understand the music."

That evening as the sun was sinking, the first swallows came back to the farmhouse. They circled the roof and settled on the eaves above Lin's head. After swooping for a drink of water in the pond, they began to build their nests.

Lin had never watched the swallows build their nests outside her home before. When she thought about it later, she realized it was because she had always been too busy practising the piano. Now she saw them pick up tiny pieces of earth in their beaks and stick them together with spit to make nests.

Day by day, the little birds flew back and forth gathering more earth and slowly they built the round mud nests where they would lay their eggs. It was hard work but wonderful work, too.

Lin sat at her piano and began to play the music. One by one, the swallows settled in a row above her head. They cocked their tiny heads as if they were listening to her and encouraging her to play. For a fraction of a second, the world seemed to stop. Lin was alone with the swallows and the music she had found so hard to play sang in the air around them. With the swallows' help she had learned to play it beautifully.

At the end of the summer, Lin won the music contest. She walked up to the stage and thanked everyone. Lin told the audience how she had watched the swallows and how much they had helped her.

"Now I understand that there are all kinds of miracles," said Lin as she bowed for the last time. "And I know there are angels everywhere."

Affirmations

· Angels can help us in different ways. Sometimes they tell us exactly what to do and sometimes they show us the way.
· If something is especially important to you, it is always worth trying to do your very best.
· It is a great feeling to be able to thank those who have helped you.

On the
Ropes

Relax, be very still and listen carefully to this story about a boy called Freddie, who grew up in a circus. His dad was the ringmaster and his mum swung high on the trapeze.

Freddie always blamed other people for his mistakes.

"Don't stand in that doorway!" shouted Dad. "The acrobats are about to come tumbling through."

"It's not my fault!" cried Freddie. "Nobody told me it was time for the show!"

On another occasion, Freddie was riding his skateboard behind the tent. WHAM! He knocked the unicycle rider right off his one-wheeled bike.

"It wasn't my fault!" said Freddie, as the clown picked himself up. "I didn't see anyone coming."

Dad was furious. "You've been told time and again not to play around here! The circus is a dangerous place."

Freddie stomped back to their caravan.

"It's not fair!" he said. Then he noticed his grandma's old

crystal ball on the shelf. It seemed to be flickering with a weird light. He picked up the ball and peered into it.

"Don't worry," said a strong, clear voice inside the glass. "You'll know when to do the right thing!"

Freddie leapt back in surprise and dropped the crystal ball on the floor. "The right thing? What does that mean? And who are you anyway?"

He scrambled to pick up the ball. There was a thin crack in it. "It's not my fault if it breaks," he thought.

Next day, Freddie had almost forgotten about the voice. He was sitting in the big top watching the show. It was his favourite bit. In a minute, Mum would swing up on to the trapeze and …

Oh no! The trapeze!

Freddie remembered that he had loosened one of the supporting ropes earlier so that he could dangle it down to the ring and tease the clowns. Now there was only one rope securely holding the trapeze when there should be two. Mum would go crashing to the ground!

Freddie leapt up. Mum was in danger, all because of him. He had to do the right thing.

"Stop!" Freddie ran into the middle of the ring.

"Don't go on the trapeze, Mum! One rope's not properly tied. It's my fault!"

The clowns came tumbling in and squirted Freddie with water. The audience roared. They thought it was a big joke. They didn't notice Freddie's dad tying the ropes up tight again. They cheered as Mum flew safely through the air.

"You were brave to own up," said Dad, in the caravan later.

"You stopped a very bad accident," said Mum.

Freddie watched a tiny light flickering in the crystal ball. "It was my fault," he said, "so I had to own up. And I dropped the crystal ball. You see, it has a crack now."

"The main thing is that you've been honest and brave, Freddie," said his mum. "I'm proud of you."

Affirmations

- Angels can help us to find the courage to "do the right thing".
- People will respect you if you own up to your mistakes.
- Don't be tempted to pretend a problem doesn't exist. Just facing up to it will make you feel better straightaway.

The Turquoise Bird

Relax, be very still and listen carefully to this story about an adventurous boy called Tom. He loved exploring new places so much that he didn't always pay attention to what he was doing. Luckily, a very beautiful angel was there to help him.

One morning Tom was jumping up and down with excitement. He was about to set off on a proper jungle expedition with his dad, who was a scientist. Tom's dad was looking for a rare purple butterfly with wings as wide as your hand. Dad travelled all over the world on his expeditions and this was the first time he had agreed to take Tom with him.

As they were setting off, Dad told him something important. "Always keep to the path and you'll stay safe."

"Why?" asked Tom.

"Because there are snakes everywhere," said Dad. "And a snake bite can be very dangerous."

But Tom wasn't really listening because a monkey was swinging through the trees above his head. And he'd never seen a monkey so close before.

All morning Tom and Dad walked along the path looking for the rare purple butterfly. They saw beetles the size of door knobs sitting on tree trunks and lizards that shone like jewels hanging by their tails from the branches. But they didn't see any butterflies.

Above them, the sun was hot and all around the shriek and buzz of the jungle was as loud as a traffic jam. Tom's dad turned a corner out of sight. In the same second, Tom saw a huge purple butterfly flutter past into the long grass beside the path. Without thinking, he pulled out his net and ran after it.

After that everything happened as if in a dream. As Tom heard his father calling out for him, a bright turquoise bird flew right past his face. It was so close Tom could feel its wings brushing his cheeks. He stopped dead in his tracks, suddenly remembering what his father had told him about never leaving the path.

And then he saw the snake – it was a deadly yellow viper with black markings. It was slithering through the grass in front of him just where he had been about to put his foot!

Tom jumped back on to the path. The turquoise bird was sitting on a branch watching him. Its eyes were pale and grey and thoughtful. Not like a bird's eyes at all. A strange stillness settled around them. Then the bird swooped down and flew around Tom's head before disappearing into the trees.

Tom ran to catch up with his father. He never told his dad what had happened. But whenever he thought of the bird's eyes and the feel of its wings on his cheek, he knew he had been saved from the snake by his guardian angel.

Affirmations

- Grown-ups have more experience than you, so you can learn and grow by listening to their advice.
- Getting carried away by excitement is fun, but you should pay attention to your inner judgment.
- You can keep yourself safe by making sure that you always follow instructions carefully.

Lily's School Play

Relax, be very still and listen carefully to this story about a girl called Lily. She learned to believe in herself with the help of an angel.

Now, imagine having to stay inside in your bedroom on a hot summer's day, even though the sun is shining and your friends are flying kites in the park outside …

Lily sighed, staring down at the script on the desk in front of her, fighting back tears. She had been horrified when Mrs Brown gave her a big part in the school play. Lily had tried to persuade her to give the part to someone else, but Mrs Brown wouldn't listen. She just said the part was perfect for Lily!

It was a play about a girl called Alice who fell down a rabbit hole into a strange, magical wonderland where amazing things happened. There was a white rabbit who talked, a cat with the biggest grin you've ever seen and a queen who shouted

"Off with his head!". Alice had all kinds of adventures. And Mrs Brown had given Lily the part of Alice – the most important person in the whole story! Lily loved the play and she really wanted to do well. But the trouble was, she just couldn't remember her lines.

The radio played quietly in the background. Sometimes it felt like music was the only thing keeping Lily sane. Tomorrow night she would be standing on a stage in front of hundreds of people, and she still kept forgetting her lines. Even Mrs Brown was worried now.

"Just practise," Mrs Brown had said. "Soon you'll be word perfect!"

Mrs Brown was quite nice – for a teacher – but Lily still didn't believe her. It didn't seem to make any difference how many times she read her lines aloud or practised them with Dad.

Lily could imagine exactly what was going to happen tomorrow evening at half past five. Standing on the stage with a dry mouth and pounding heart, she would wait for the curtains to open. The whole audience would be staring at her – and all the lines she'd struggled to learn would simply disappear from her head. That was what had happened last night, at the dress rehearsal. Why would it be any different for the real performance?

The letters on the page in front of Lily blurred before her eyes, making no sense at all.

"It's no use," Lily said aloud. "I might as well not bother. I'll never remember these lines!" Just as she spoke, the song playing on the radio was drowned in a flood of static.

"Great," she muttered, fiddling with the aerial. "This is the last thing I need."

Lily couldn't find the radio signal again, however much she twisted the aerial.

"Argh!" She stood up from the desk, walked across the room and threw herself down on the bed.

She looked up through the skylight.

"I give up!" she said. "Who cares about a stupid play, anyway?"

She watched the birds wheel and dive in the blue sky. The buzzing static from the radio was driving her mad. She wanted to switch the stupid thing off. But somehow Lily couldn't even make herself get off the bed and walk across the room. Suddenly she felt so very tired. What was the point in even trying? Lily knew she was going to panic and forget every single line she'd managed to cram into her head. Mrs Brown would have to take her place on the stage tomorrow night.

"Hey, what are you doing just lying there?" The DJ's voice sliced through the airways like a knife. Lily jumped up, staring at the radio on the far side of the room. The buzzing had faded completely. What strange station was the radio tuned to now? And who was that weird DJ?

"Why are you giving up now?" he asked. Outside the window, a bird was singing.

Lily froze where she was sitting. Was the DJ really talking to her?

"You've done so much extra practice," the DJ went on. "Think about it, Lily. This is the first time you've ever had a big part in a school play. No wonder you panicked at the dress rehearsal. But Mrs Brown picked you for a reason — you're brilliant! Things will be different tomorrow, you wait and see."

Lily was tempted to pinch herself, like people did in stories. Was she asleep and dreaming? She knew she wasn't. The DJ on the radio really was talking to her!

"You can do it, Lily. You just have to believe it yourself." The DJ's voice was so calm and soothing that, even though Lily should have been terrified, she felt warm and comforted – excited, even. This was magic – or something else equally wonderful – and it was happening to her.

That very second, the buzzing static flooded the room again. Then suddenly music blasted out from the radio, halfway through a song.

Lily sat on the bed, staring up out of the window. Who was that DJ and why had he decided to help her? Had she imagined the whole thing? Then she realized that it didn't matter. She smiled.

"I can do it," she told herself. "I CAN do it!"

Affirmations

- Angels help you to have confidence in yourself – and the more confidence you have, the more you can achieve.
- Sometimes you have to try and fail a few times before you succeed. It's through failing that you learn how to do something better.
- Persevering can take a lot of courage, but will be worth the effort in the end.

The Old Man
and the See-saw

Relax, be very still and listen carefully to this story about two selfish princesses called Tiara and Topaz.

Princess Tiara and Princess Topaz lived in a castle. They had everything they wanted, but they wanted more. They were always arguing because they didn't know how to share or play together.

Although they were twins, the two princesses were completely different. Tiara was tall and chubby with long, thick black hair. Topaz was short and skinny with curly hair the colour of carrots. Tiara liked doing tough things like pushing her sister into the castle moat, while Topaz liked doing sneaky things like hiding in a tree and dropping flour on her sister's head.

One day, their father, King Phoenix, banged his walking stick on the floor. "If you don't stop arguing and start getting on with each other," he cried, "I will leave my kingdom to your cousin Cecil instead of you!"

Both princesses were horrified.

"But it's MY kingdom," cried Princess Tiara.

"No! It's MINE!" shouted Princess Topaz.

Then Tiara said, "Cecil is a weed. I don't like him."

"I don't like him either," said Topaz.

"See," said Tiara. "We agree on something."

"Yeah," said Topaz, looking suspiciously at her sister.

"That's not good enough," said King Phoenix. "If you don't learn how to get on and share things by sunset, Prince Cecil will get the kingdom, not you two."

All that afternoon, the two princesses tried to do things together in the castle gardens, but they found it impossible. Tiara offered her sister a sandwich from her picnic box, but it turned out she had already eaten the filling.

Topaz finished off the lemonade before her sister had even had a sip. Slowly but surely, the sun began to set.

"What are we going to do?" wailed Princess Tiara.

"It's all your fault," shouted Princess Topaz.

A sound of hammering came through the trees.

"What's that?" demanded Princess Topaz.

"How should I know?" snapped Princess Tiara.

They ran to look. Behind a hedge they found a strange old man with shining grey hair, wearing a long white robe. Nearby a long plank was balanced on a block.

"What on earth is that?" asked Tiara.

"A see-saw," said the old man. "I built it specially for you to share. One sits at one end and one at the other, then you push up with your feet."

There was something about his voice that made both princesses do what he said right away.

It was AMAZING! The princesses soared up and down in the air. It was the first time they had ever played together properly and they had the best time ever.

That night they told their father about their adventure. King Phoenix hugged his daughters. "That man must have been an angel," he cried. "Only an angel could have made you two learn how to share."

Affirmations

⬦⬦⬦⬦⬦⬦⬦⬦⬦⬦⬦⬦⬦⬦⬦⬦⬦⬦⬦

- Everyone has a good side, no matter how annoying they may seem at first.
- Squabbling over little things doesn't just make us unhappy, it also upsets all the people around us. Try to be generous.
- Being close to someone – such as a sister, a brother or a friend – is the most important thing in the world.

Light in
the Dark

Relax, be very still and listen carefully to this story about a boy called Jason, who was frightened of the dark.

One day, Jason's Uncle Jim asked him to go on a caving trip. Jason was really excited — he had never been caving before, and he agreed right away. But as the day of the trip got closer, Jason started to worry. He had never told anyone, but he was scared of the dark!

"You will be perfectly safe with me," said Uncle Jim. He gave Jason a helmet with a lamp on the front and a flashlight to put in his pocket. "These are brand-new lights and I've tested the batteries, so you needn't worry about the dark."

But Jason felt his stomach go wobbly the moment they squeezed through a narrow entrance into the first cave. He had known it would be very dark, but Jason hadn't realized that without a flashlight he wouldn't even be able to see his hand in front of his face!

"Everything OK?" called Uncle Jim.

"Er, great," said Jason, trying to sound brave.

They crawled through a tunnel and came into a huge cavern. In the light from his helmet, Jason saw pointed things that looked like melting candles hanging from the ceiling. The same shapes were rising up from the ground.

"Those are stalactites and stalagmites," said Uncle Jim. "They're made by water drops." Sure enough, the sound of dripping water echoed all around.

Jason crawled into another tunnel after his uncle. It was very muddy and he slipped – and an awful thing happened! The lamp on his helmet went out.

"Oh no!" thought Jason. "At least I've got the flashlight." But when he felt for it, it wasn't there!

Bang! Bang! Bang! Jason's heart pounded in his chest. It was completely black all around him. He had to clench his fists to stop himself from shouting out loud. What was he going to do?

Suddenly, a flickering ball of light appeared out of nowhere. Fireflies! Some flew around his head and others flew into the tunnel so he could see his way forward.

Jason had seen fireflies before. Sometimes he caught them in a jam jar when he went camping. But fireflies live in woods, not caves. Where had they come from?

More fireflies fluttered into the tunnel and it grew brighter and brighter.

"Are you all right, Jason?" Uncle Jim was calling him from some distance away. He sounded worried.

Jason looked at the beautiful flickering light that shone all around him. He realized his heart had stopped pounding and he no longer felt frightened at all.

"I'm fine, Uncle Jim," shouted Jason and he almost burst out laughing. "I've got angels looking after me!"

As Jason turned the corner, the fireflies disappeared as quickly as they had arrived. The lamp on his helmet came on again. He looked down and saw his flashlight on the ground.

This time, Jason didn't ask why or how. He picked up the flashlight and whispered a huge thank you to the tiny angels who had helped him.

Affirmations

⬦⬦⬦⬦⬦⬦⬦⬦⬦⬦⬦⬦⬦⬦⬦

- Even when your situation looks bad, help is often close by. Stay hopeful.
- Taking deep breaths and trying to stay calm helps when we are very afraid.
- It is OK to admit that you are afraid of things. Sometimes just admitting your fear can help you to overcome it.

The Smallest
Giant

Relax, be very still and listen carefully to this story about a young giant called Tim. Although Tim was a giant, he felt very small until, one day, he helped a tiny little girl with the voice of an angel.

Tim was as tall as a tree. Each hand was as big as a bicycle wheel, his nose was as long as a playground slide and he wore size 88½ shoes.

But, although he'd look huge to you or me, Tim was the youngest and smallest of all the giant clan.

"Where's Tiny Tim?" his friends would tease.

"I don't know," they'd laugh, even though Tim was standing right beside them. "He's so small, we can't even see him!"

The other young giants could stride over the mountain, down the valley and through the sea in just a few BIG steps. But poor Tim's legs weren't so long. He had to skid down the mountain and swim through the deep parts of the sea instead of just wading through. He was always the last to reach the giant playground on the opposite shore.

By the time he got there, the giants were already tired of the playground. They were bored. They were looking for something else to do.

"Let's squash Tiny Tim!" roared Barry Bigfoot.

"Let's roll him into a ball and throw him around," grinned Thick-necked Ned.

"Please can we dress him up in tiny clothes and play dolls with him," begged Long-legged Lucy.

"No!" said the boy giants. "We don't want to play dolls with him!"

So they jumped on Tim instead. They chased him. They pulled him and pushed him. And all because he was smaller than they were.

But, as summer wore on, even picking on Tiny Tim was no fun any more.

"What shall we do?" groaned Long-legged Lucy. "I'm bored with everything."

"There's nothing to do," moaned Barry Bigfoot.

"Unless ..." said Thick-necked Ned, "Unless we go and bully the humans!"

"Brilliant!" cried Tim. "Let's go, straight away!"

Humans are really little, he thought. At last, I won't be the smallest one of all. I can have some fun. I can pick on someone even tinier than me!

The giants bounded off across the countryside, with Tim doing his best to keep up. In no time at all, they reached a human village.

But the village was deserted.

"There's nobody here," said Long-legged Lucy.

"They must have heard us coming and run away!" said Barry Bigfoot. He picked up a bicycle as if it was a tiny toy in his hand.

"How annoying!" groaned Thick-necked Ned. "Now we'll just have to bully Tim as usual."

"Wait!" said Tim. "I can see a human. A really tiny one. Down there! Look!"

A little girl was trying to hide behind a street light. She had golden hair and the bluest eyes Tim had ever seen.

"Let's squash her!" shouted Thick-necked Ned, shaking his fist.

"Let's stamp on her!" roared Barry Bigfoot.

But Tim saw that the tiny girl was very frightened. He knelt down to get a closer look.

"Please don't hurt me," she begged. Her voice was small and very quiet. But it was the sweetest voice that Tim had ever heard.

Tim knew that he had to get rid of the other giants or they would squash the little girl.

"Look!" he said, pointing in the opposite direction. "I saw some more humans over there!"

"Let's get 'em!" shouted Long-legged Lucy.

The giants ran down the street. Tim gently picked up the little girl and popped her into the low branches of a tree.

"Hide there, till your friends come back," he whispered. "Stay quiet and you'll be safe!"

The next moment the giants reappeared. They were not happy.

"I didn't see anything," roared Barry Bigfoot.

"There's nobody there at all!" shouted Thick-necked Ned.

"Sorry!" said Tim, "I was sure I saw something. Got to get off now — Mum's expecting me!" He started to run away.

A tiny giggle came from the branches of the tree. But the other giants were grumbling too loud to hear.

"Now you've lost my tiny doll-girl!" boomed Long-legged

Lucy, searching behind the street light. "I was going to keep her in a box!"

The giants were so furious they chased Tim all the way home.

Early next morning, Tim tiptoed into the human village alone. He guessed at once where the little girl lived – a house where the sunlight hit the windows and made them shine like gold.

"I'm so sorry I frightened you yesterday," he whispered. "I know how it feels to be picked on because you are small."

The little girl pulled back the curtains and smiled at him.

"Thank you for helping me," she said, in her sweet voice.

"Who are you?" Tim asked, but she had already vanished. Tim never saw her again but he never forgot her smile or her lovely voice – the voice of an angel.

Affirmations

- When you help someone, you might just be helping an angel in disguise.
- Don't be scared of making friends because someone looks different from you or comes from another country. There are wonderful experiences to be had.
- Don't pick on other people because you are having a bad time. Deep inside you know it's better to be kind and friendly.

The Perfect Picture

Relax, be very still and listen carefully to this story about a boy called Emmett, who loved to take photographs. Our story begins as he was sitting on a log near the campsite, peering through the viewfinder of his camera.

"Come on, Emmett!" His sister, Ginny, was waving her towel. "Aren't you coming swimming in the lake?"

"Later," he said. "I want to photograph the stag."

"You've been sitting here for hours already," sighed Ginny. "You're so boring since you got that camera."

"If I sit still, I might be in luck," Emmett whispered. "The stag sometimes comes to the stream to drink."

"BORING!" groaned Ginny.

"Shhhhhh!" he said. "Go swimming. I'm staying here."

He took a snapshot of her scowling.

"Fine!" she said. "Who needs brothers anyway?" Ginny ran on down the hill.

Before long, he could hear her splashing

with their cousins in the lake, shrieking with laughter. They always screamed when they jumped into the freezing water. Then they would climb onto the rocks to warm up in the sun.

Emmett thought how great it would be to dive-bomb into the water. But he knew he'd have to wait if he wanted a picture of the stag. The creature would come to drink when he was ready. Not before.

By lunchtime, there was still no sign of the stag.

"Come on!" shouted Ginny as she ran by, dripping wet. "We're cooking sausages on the fire."

Emmett was tempted. He loved sausages and he was starving! He'd eaten his sandwich hours ago. But he stayed still. The stag might come, now the woods were quiet.

Emmett stayed on his log all that afternoon while the others were playing tag in the hay field. His back ached. It was chilly in the shade. And he was getting bored.

He was sitting so still, a dragonfly landed right beside him. He got a wonderful photograph of it. But all he wanted was to see the stag.

"This is hopeless!" Emmett said, as time dragged on. He kicked a pile of leaves. "I've missed all the fun for nothing!"

And then Emmett saw him! The stag was drinking at the stream. Suddenly he raised his head and looked straight at Emmett. They stared at each other for a moment, transfixed.

Perhaps it was the way the sun shone through the trees, but it seemed as if the stag was made of shimmering gold. His magnificent antlers spread out above him like wings. He looked like an angel.

All the aches went from Emmett's body and the hours of waiting slipped away.

He focused his lens. Click.

The sound of the camera must have startled the stag. When Emmett looked up again, he was gone.

But, now, whenever Emmett looks at his photograph of that magnificent stag, he is proud that he was patient. It was worth the wait!

Affirmations

◇◇◇◇◇◇◇◇◇◇◇◇◇◇◇◇◇◇

- If you are strong and patient enough to see a project through to the end, you will be rewarded.
- It can be hard to do something different from everybody else, especially if they are having fun, but following your own heart is the biggest adventure.
- When you have to wait for something, you will appreciate it more.

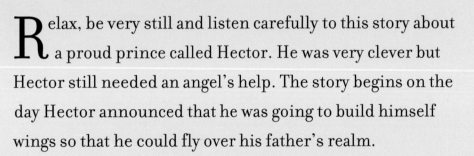

The Proud Prince

Relax, be very still and listen carefully to this story about a proud prince called Hector. He was very clever but Hector still needed an angel's help. The story begins on the day Hector announced that he was going to build himself wings so that he could fly over his father's realm.

Hector's father, King Richard, was worried by his son's plan. "You are my only son and I need your help to run the kingdom," he said. "This is a crazy, dangerous thing to do."

"Nonsense, Father," replied Hector, as he glued long white feathers onto strips of wood. "These wings will lift me up just like a bird." Hector stepped back to admire his clever work. "I have never failed before," he boasted.

"There's always a first time," replied King Richard. But he knew that there was no point in arguing. Prince Hector had done exactly what he wanted ever since he was a baby.

The night before his first flight, Prince Hector had the strangest dream. An old woman dressed in a long smock made of leaves appeared in front of him. Her face was brown and lined like the bark of a tree and it seemed to Prince Hector that her gnarled arms and hands were like branches and twigs.

She looked into Hector's eyes, as if she could see into his mind. "Only birds fly," she said. "You are a prince. Your duty is to help your father."

Prince Hector pushed the old woman from his mind. "What a silly dream," he said and went back to sleep.

Before dawn, while everyone was still in bed, Hector tucked his wings under his arm and left the castle. As the sun rose, he stood on the edge of a cliff overlooking the sea and strapped his wings to his back. Then he stretched out his arms and jumped.

The wind held him up and he flapped his wings to turn around and fly over his kingdom. "I can fly! I can fly!" he shouted into the air.

Then everything went wrong. Prince Hector felt himself falling through the air, faster and faster. The side of the cliff rushed past him and far below the sea churned over rocks sharp as spikes.

As he fell, Prince Hector remembered the old lady in his dream and he wished he had listened to her warning. Now his poor old father would die without an heir and the kingdom would fall apart.

Suddenly, there was a great tug as his wings caught on a branch of a tree that grew out of the cliff face. Hector found himself dangling like a rag doll over the crashing sea. His feet felt a narrow ledge and he wrapped his arms around the branch and held on as tightly as he could.

Perhaps it was the lined, brown bark close to his face or the feel of the wood – but Prince Hector knew that the old woman in his dream had somehow turned herself into the tree that had saved him. She was his guardian angel and he should have taken her advice.

Hector whispered "Thank you," into the branches as he pulled himself up and climbed the cliff to safety. From that day on, Hector did his duty as a prince.

Affirmations

- Helpful messages can come to us in surprising ways – even in dreams.
- No matter how clever we think we are, we can always learn more from those who are wiser than ourselves.
- Thinking what is best for other people, not just for ourselves, helps us work out the right thing to do.

The Mysterious Cowboy

Relax, be very still and listen carefully to this story about a girl called Sadie, who was feeling very hurt and angry. She met the most unlikely angel in the most unlikely place – and found out all about forgiveness.

Sadie's father ran a restaurant and bar. One day Sadie was sitting by herself in her favourite corner. She watched Dad's assistant Billy polish the tables before opening time. Sadie glared at the long bar, the tables and chairs. It was five thirty – still half an hour before people would start to arrive. Sadie knew that later that night, when she was in her bedroom in the apartment above the restaurant, she would be able to hear grown-ups shouting and laughing into the early hours of the morning. Some nights there was live music, too – usually Country and Western, Dad's favourite.

Sadie's bedroom smelled of fresh paint. Dad and his new girlfriend, Lucinda, had decorated

it for her and put up lots of new posters. But Sadie
still didn't want to be there. It was all Dad's fault that
she had to stay in a pokey bedroom where she couldn't
even sleep because of the noise from downstairs. He was
the one who had run away with a new girlfriend. He was the
reason that, last Saturday, Sadie's mum had got married
again. Now Sadie was stuck with that annoying Lucinda
while Mum and her new husband were on their honeymoon.

The restaurant door swung open. Dad and Lucinda
strolled in hand in hand. Dad was carrying Lucinda's
shopping bags. Sadie frowned at them.

Dad smiled. "Wouldn't you like to do something more
interesting than just sitting there?" he asked.

"We've got all those DVDs upstairs, Sadie!" chipped in
Lucinda, smiling too. "Maybe you and I could watch *Fairy
Princesses* together later?"

"No thanks," Sadie said, turning away. Sadie liked
wearing grubby jeans, reading books and climbing trees in
the garden at home. "I'd rather pull out my teeth one
by one than watch *Fairy Princesses*!" she thought.

"Oh, OK then," replied Lucinda looking upset
as she headed for the door that led upstairs.

Dad shook his head at Sadie. "You could at

least make an effort. Lucinda's trying really
hard to be your friend."

Sadie could hardly believe her ears. Dad
was the one in the wrong. Nothing could
change what he had done, but here he was trying
to blame her!

"It's your fault!" she told him. "I hate you!" Dad's
face crumpled and Sadie thought he was going to cry.
He followed Lucinda out the door.

Sadie had never felt more alone. Billy was at the far
end of the room, laying out cutlery on the
tables. She hoped he hadn't overheard.
A single tear trailed down her face.

Sadie was very angry with Dad. She couldn't
forget how, after he'd gone, Mum had cried
whenever she thought Sadie couldn't hear her.
They'd worried a lot about money, too.

Sadie looked up as the door opened again.

Billy, still steadily putting out glasses, didn't
seem to notice. A tall, skinny old man loped in, wearing a
cowboy hat and boots, and carrying a battered guitar case.
He came and sat down at the stool nearest to Sadie and
touched the rim of his hat. He nodded at her.

"What's a man got to do to get a cold drink in this place?"
He smiled.

Sadie smiled back. She couldn't help it. "You look just
like a cowboy!" The words flew out of her mouth before she
could stop them.

"Well, maybe I am," he replied.

"Are you playing here tonight?" Sadie asked, looking
at the guitar. "If you are, you get free drinks."

"That's good news," said the cowboy. He had a long,
droopy grey moustache. "I guess I am playing here tonight.
Me and this old guitar, we've travelled many a long road."

Sadie went to the refrigerator behind the bar. She took
out a cold bottle of lemonade and passed it to the cowboy.

"Thank you, Miss." He tipped his hat to her
again. "I'm a poor man, so all I can give in return
is words."

Sadie stared, blinking. The old cowboy was
surrounded by a strange, silvery glow.

"It's time to move on, Sadie," the cowboy said.
"Forgive your dad. He's truly sorry that you
were hurt."

"What are you talking about?" Sadie
demanded. And how did he know her name?

The man smiled and the silvery glow brightened — Sadie had to hold her hands over her eyes.

A door slammed.

"Sadie?" called her dad.

Sadie blinked. The cowboy — if that's what he really was — had gone.

Her dad was standing in the doorway, looking sad. Sadie felt lighter, as if she'd put down a heavy bag. She wasn't angry any more. Was the cowboy right? Maybe it was time to forgive Dad.

"I need a hug, Dad," she said, rushing over to him. And he scooped her up and twirled her around just as he'd always done.

Affirmations

- Life doesn't always work out as we would like — it's good to look for the positive in everything that happens.
- Getting angry is a natural, healthy way to react when someone hurts our feelings, so long as we don't let the anger last too long.
- Anger can make it hard to forgive someone, but you always feel much better once you let the anger go.

The Honest Shepherd

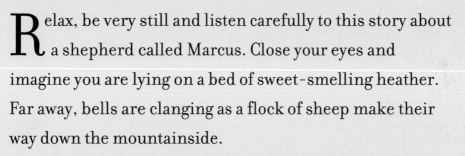

Relax, be very still and listen carefully to this story about a shepherd called Marcus. Close your eyes and imagine you are lying on a bed of sweet-smelling heather. Far away, bells are clanging as a flock of sheep make their way down the mountainside.

Marcus spent his days looking after his sheep. But one awful night a pack of wolves killed his flock. Now he had nothing left except the clothes he wore and his shepherd's crook. The next day he left the mountain to find work.

As Marcus drew near to the town, a man on a horse trotted past. The man wore a fine cloak and a fur hat. As he called out, "Good day!", a pheasant fluttered up from the bushes. The man's horse reared and galloped on down the path.

When the dust cleared, Marcus saw a red leather bag on the ground. He picked it up. It was full of gold coins! He shouted for the man to stop, but the horse was disappearing around a bend in the path.

95

Marcus counted the money. There was enough to buy a flock of sheep and some blankets for the winter. He could keep it all and go to another valley. No one would know. Marcus felt his fingers close around the bag.

"Is all that money yours?" asked a little voice.

A small boy was sitting by the path. His face shone under his curly blond hair and his blue eyes seemed to read the thoughts in Marcus's head.

Marcus felt dizzy. He was an honest shepherd. As he opened his mouth to answer the boy's question, he knew he couldn't steal the rich man's purse.

"Of course not," he said. "How could a poor shepherd have so many gold coins?" He smiled at the boy in relief. "A rich man riding by dropped the bag. I'll find him in the market place and give it back to him."

It was easy to find a tall man wearing a cloak and fur hat. His name was Maximilian Astor and he was very pleased to have his purse returned.

"I see you are a shepherd," he said, giving Marcus a coin to thank him. "Where are your sheep?"

Marcus told him how he had come to find a job.

"Look no further!" cried Maximilian. "I came to this market to find an honest shepherd. I offer good pay and somewhere to live – and a chance to build up your own flock again. Will you accept?"

"I would be honoured," said Marcus and both men laughed with delight as they shook hands on the agreement.

At that moment Marcus caught sight of the bright-faced boy. He seemed to shimmer in the light.

Marcus felt a shiver pass through his body. He knew now that the little boy was an angel who had saved him from stealing the purse and making a terrible mistake.

"You look pale, my friend!" said Maximilian, putting his arm around Marcus's shoulder. "Come! We shall have food and wine to celebrate our new friendship!" And together they made their way happily to the inn.

Affirmations

· Angels help us to resist when we are tempted to do something bad.
· Honesty is always the best policy. Even if we don't have much ourselves, it makes sense to try to return lost property to its owner.
· Doing the right thing will make you happy – it's a reward in itself, even if no one else ever knows what you have done.

The Magic Trick

Relax, be very still and listen carefully to this story about Edmund, who was scared of making new friends. His parents had decided to move house – right from one side of the country to the other. Edmund wasn't pleased.

"But Mum," he said, "I won't know anyone at school!"

Edmund's mother just patted his head and went on packing boxes. "You'll be all right," she said. "I know you're shy but you'll soon make friends. How exciting it'll be."

Edmund wasn't excited. His insides churned with terror like a pair of socks in a washing machine.

They moved as planned. Edmund's mother parked beside a cottage down a long, winding lane. His father said, "Look at the garden and those fields! We'll have a great time here."

"What does he know?" Edmund thought. "He's not the one starting a new school on Monday."

The weekend shot past in a flurry of cardboard boxes. On Monday morning, Edmund dragged his feet as he went to school. He stared at the floor as the teacher told everyone who he was.

"I'm sure you'll all make Edmund feel very welcome," she said.

At playtime, he was surrounded by a crowd of children. "Where have you come from?" they asked. "Have you got any brothers or sisters?"

He whispered his answers so quietly that the other children couldn't hear him. Eventually, they drifted away.

When Edmund got home his parents were hunting for the dustpan. He didn't want to worry them by saying how much he hated his new school, so he helped them look. He started in the bathroom — and that was where he found a shoebox, under the sink.

There was something inside, only it wasn't a dustpan. It was a little, shimmery, old lady, like a tiny granny made of silver light! She sat in the box, smiling up at him.

"I've been waiting for you, young man," she said.

"Why?" Edmund asked, when he'd stopped gawping.

The little old lady laughed. "To tell you about my magic trick — the friend-making one. I know a few good tricks, believe me. Smile at the first person who talks to you tomorrow, a big toothy grin. They won't be able to resist."

"It'll never work," Edmund whispered.

"Try it or how can you know?" the old lady replied.

Then she disappeared in a puff of lavender smoke.

At playtime the next morning Edmund huddled by a wall.

He stared at his feet as boys played football nearby.

"It's going to hit the window!" someone shouted.

Suddenly Edmund was flat on his back, gasping for air.

The football had hit him right in the stomach. Tears came

to his eyes, just as a freckled face appeared above him.

"Sorry about that," the boy said.

"A big toothy grin," Edmund thought. "Just try it!"

So he smiled. "Don't worry about it. Silly place to be

standing anyway."

The freckled boy smiled back. "Are you playing, then?"

Edmund's smile grew wider still. "Yes!" he said.

Affirmations

⬦⬦⬦⬦⬦⬦⬦⬦⬦⬦⬦⬦⬦⬦⬦⬦⬦

· It's natural to be afraid of new things, but everyone — even shy people —
can learn to cope with big changes.

· Making new friends isn't always easy, but most people respond well to
a smile. It's a good way to start.

· True bravery can be found even in everyday situations.

Dad's Big Day

Relax, be very still and listen carefully to this story about a brother and a sister and their Dad's funny-looking old car.

Mum woke the children early. "Today's the big day," she said. "Dad is up and dressed already, and raring to go!"

It was the day of the car rally. Dad had been looking forward to the race for months. This year Mum had to go to work, so it would just be the three of them in the car – Dad, Daniel and Olivia. The race would start in the town square, then they would drive along the coast road all the way to the finishing line at the lighthouse.

"Not that we'll ever reach the finishing line," yawned Olivia, sitting up in bed.

"Never!" agreed Daniel.

Mum put her finger to her lips. "Don't let Dad hear you say that," she whispered. "He's worked really hard to get Lulu ready for the race this year."

Lulu was Dad's old car. And she really was very old. In fact, she was falling apart. But she was still Dad's pride and joy. He called her "Lovely Lulu" and worked on her every weekend.

Through the bedroom window, the children could see Dad giving Lulu a final polish.

"Remember last year?" said Daniel.

Olivia groaned. "How could I forget? It was SO embarrassing. Lulu broke down before we reached the town square. We didn't even start the race!"

But this year Lulu chugged into the town square in good time for the start of the rally. Dad's big tool box took up the whole of the front seat.

"Just in case of any little problems," said Dad. He patted the front of the car. "But there won't be any."

"No!" whispered Daniel. "There won't be any little problems. But there might be some BIG ones!"

"Like the time Lulu's front wheel fell off," hissed Olivia.

"Or when her exhaust pipe exploded," groaned Daniel.

Dad didn't hear them. He was too busy polishing Lulu's hub cabs.

"There you are, Old Girl!" he said, talking to the car. "You look grand."

He took his cloth and polished the tiny silver angel that stood on the very front of the car.

"Lulu is a Rolls Royce!" he reminded the children. "She may be old and battered now, but in her day she would have been the finest, fastest, fanciest car on the road!"

Olivia closed her eyes and tried to imagine what Lulu would have looked like when she was shiny and new. For a moment she could almost see her, glimmering silver and bright.

"Remember to call her 'Lovely Lulu!'" said Dad, climbing into the driver's seat. "If we give her plenty of encouragement, she's sure to win."

"Come on, Lovely Lulu," muttered the children.

"Louder!" cried Dad.

Olivia nudged Daniel. Dad had worked so hard. They should try their best to sound confident.

"COME ON, LOVELY LULU!" they cheered.

"What a heap of old junk!" said a voice behind them.

Daniel turned round and his heart sank. It was Sam, the coolest boy in school. Daniel didn't want Sam to see him in Dad's scruffy old car. Sam always had the latest, most expensive stuff. And Daniel could see that Sam's dad's car

was no exception. It was bright red and sporty.
It looked more like a fighter jet than a car.

"Wow!" said Daniel. He'd have given anything
to ride in a car like that.

Dad turned on Lulu's engine. She spluttered and shook.
Black smoke poured out the exhaust and the silver angel
on the front of the car disappeared in a thick, black cloud.
Olivia and Daniel couldn't stop themselves from coughing.

"You two should come with us," laughed Sam's dad.
"You'll never make it to the lighthouse in that broken-down
old thing."

Daniel was so excited he didn't notice that Sam's
dad had called Lulu a "broken-down old thing".

He bounded forward. "Can I really come in your
car?" he shouted. This was great! The fast sports
car was sure to win the race. But then he looked
back at Lulu. The smoke had cleared and the
whole car seemed to shimmer. Daniel even thought
he glimpsed the tiny angel flap her wings.

"I understand if you want to go," said Dad, but he looked
really sad.

"No!" said Daniel. "I'd rather ride with you." He knew
the race would be spoilt for Dad if he went in Sam's car.

"Lulu may be old," said Olivia, "but she's lovely. And she's ours."

"Climb in, then!" said Dad, beaming. "The race is about to begin!"

Lulu broke down five times before they reached the finishing line. By the time they got to the lighthouse, all the other cars had gone home. Sam and his dad had sped past hours ago, clutching a big, gold winner's cup.

"Never mind!" said Olivia, as they spread a picnic rug on the grass and stared out to sea. "Look at the sunset!"

"We'd have missed that view if we'd got here any earlier," said Daniel.

"Well done, Lovely Lulu!" they all cheered. And the angel glowed in the sun.

Affirmations

- We don't always know what we really want. Angels can help us to find out.
- Try to stop and think before acting. It's always good to think about other people's feelings.
- Making someone else happy often makes us happy ourselves.

Odd One Out

Relax, be very still and listen carefully to this story about a girl called Cara, who was being bullied by her step-sister. She didn't know what to do, until someone special helped her while she was on holiday. So, close your eyes and feel the hot sun on your shoulders, just as it beat down on Cara on the day our story begins.

Cara had been waiting with her family outside the museum for what seemed like hours. She was fed up. It was bad enough that her mum and her step-father, David, had decided that they were all going on holiday to Italy together. Only the thought of long white beaches and glittering swimming pools had made up for the prospect of a holiday with her horrible step-sister, Imogen. She certainly hadn't imagined wasting days in dusty old museums.

"Ow!" cried Cara, as Imogen shoved past, treading on her foot. Imogen was always doing things like that, when she thought that no one was looking.

Cara watched as Imogen went up to David and took his hand. David put his other arm around Mum's shoulders. Cara stood behind, feeling left out as usual.

She was relieved when Mum finally said, "Great, they're letting us in now."

The outside of the museum reminded Cara of a wedding cake — white and towering — but inside it was cool and dark. It took her eyes a moment to adjust. The crowd shuffled onward, Cara and her family among them. Imogen shoved past Cara again, this time pinching her arm hard and so sneakily that no one else saw. Cara had tears in her eyes. What was Imogen's problem? Why couldn't she just leave Cara alone?

It was tempting to get Imogen into trouble, but Cara knew that if she did, Imogen would get back at her as soon as they were alone. And what was the point anyway? The four of them were stuck with each other.

"Wow," David said. "Isn't that amazing? The guidebook says that this museum was once the home of a nobleman. To show how rich he was, he paid a famous artist to make a painting that covered the whole ceiling of this hall!"

Cara sighed and looked up. It was true. The ceiling was amazing — one enormous painting of a sky filled with cupids, angels and saints in bright robes with shining haloes.

Sunlight streamed from a tiny window near the roof to light up a beautiful red-haired angel. She hovered alone at the edge of the painting. Her huge, swan-like wings were spread out behind her and long white robes flowed around her feet. For a moment, it really looked like the angel was flying.

"Don't be an idiot," Cara thought. "It's just a painting. I wish I was an angel and could fly away from Imogen!"

Cara glanced at her step-sister. Imogen stood between Mum and David, chatting cheerfully about where they were going for lunch. They made a perfect group of three. Mum always looked beautiful, with her cool linen dresses and silver bracelets. David and Imogen were blonde and suntanned. Cara stared down at her scruffy dress and pale, chubby legs.

"I'm never going to fit in," she thought. "Maybe I should just go and live with Dad."

But Cara knew that was never going to happen. Cara's father was a businessman who flew around the world several times a year. He had an expensive apartment filled with

precious objects, but there was no room for Cara there. Tears spilled down her face.

"Imogen's jealous of you, you know. That's why she's so horrible to you," whispered a musical voice.

Cara raised her head and gasped. Through her tears she saw the red-headed angel standing right in front of her, bare feet on the marble floor. The angel's wings lifted slightly and the thick white feathers stirred a breeze that cooled Cara's face.

The angel smiled. "You wouldn't believe how fascinating humans are to watch. Sometimes I like to help — when I see someone really miserable."

"Wh … what are you talking about?" Cara glanced around the hall. No one else had noticed the angel. They were all still staring up at the painted ceiling or peering into their guidebooks.

"Well, look at your step-sister," said the angel, her red hair glowing like fire. "It seems to you as if she's got everything. But really she's scared her dad won't love her as much now you and your mother are around."

Cara stared at the angel, unable to speak. Could this really be happening?

"Oh yes," the angel went on. "Imogen is terrified that you're going to take her dad away. Did you know that she lies awake worrying about it every night? Things aren't always as they seem at first. Maybe Imogen needs your help."

A second later the angel standing before Cara had vanished. Cara blinked. Had she imagined the whole thing?

"Go on, help Imogen," a voice whispered in Cara's mind. She looked up. The red-haired angel was back high on the wall, still watching.

After a moment Cara took a deep breath. She had made up her mind. She would get to know Imogen better, so that they could be a real family. Cara put on her best smile and walked up to her step-sister.

Affirmations

◇◇◇◇◇◇◇◇◇◇◇◇◇◇◇◇

- Angels can help us to find the strength to stand up to bullies.
- Coping with a bully is easier if you remember that bullies usually act that way because they are afraid of something.
- A good way of making up a quarrel with someone is to try imagining yourself in their shoes.

The Kind
Monkey

Relax, be very still and listen carefully to this story about a boy called Emeka, who lived in Nigeria in Africa. Now, imagine you are lying in the shade under a leafy tree. A warm breeze ruffles your hair and you can hear birds calling in the branches.

Emeka's name meant "someone who does great deeds". But this particular day Emeka was not living up to his name. He was grumpy. He wanted his mother to read to him, even though she was tired because she was about to have a baby.

"Go outside and play with your cousins," said Emeka's grandmother. "Let your mother be."

But Emeka kept pushing his book at his mother. At last his grandmother took him by the hand and led him out of the hut. "Off you go for a walk," she said firmly. "And don't come back with that grumpy face."

Emeka stomped into the jungle, kicking the earth and hitting the trees with a stick. The truth was that he didn't

115

want a new baby in his family. He liked having his mother and father and grandmother all to himself.

Suddenly, Emeka heard a rustle in the branches. He looked up and saw a pure white monkey with a tiny sleeping baby clasped to her chest. Another young monkey was holding her hand. It looked like the baby's older sister. He watched as the mother pulled down two mangoes and gave one to her daughter. The mother groomed her daughter's fur and they ate the juicy fruit together.

Emeka felt a lump in his throat. Deep down he was afraid that when the baby was born, his mother wouldn't love him anymore. But as he watched the monkey mother groom her daughter's fur, Emeka realized he'd got everything wrong. His mother would never stop loving him. She had more than enough love to give to him and the new baby as well.

Now Emeka felt guilty for pestering his mother when he knew she wanted to sleep. Staring up at the monkey, he saw her give him a long, thoughtful look. Then she reached for a handful of mangoes and carefully dropped the fruit on the ground. The monkeys disappeared among the leaves.

Emeka returned home with the mangoes. His mother was delighted with them – mangoes were her favourite fruit. "How did you get them?" she asked.

Emeka told her how the monkey had picked the mangoes for him. Then he took his mother's hand and said he was sorry for being selfish.

Emeka's mother smiled. "That monkey was a kind angel," she said.

"But it was just a monkey in the jungle," said Emeka.

"It doesn't matter," said his mother. "Angels come in all shapes and sizes."

That night, Emeka's mother had her baby. It was a girl and she called her Ebele.

"Why did you give her that name?" asked Emeka.

"Because Ebele means kindness," said his mother. "Now you will always remember the angel who helped you."

Affirmations

- Sometimes angels show us the truth without speaking, and if we think hard we will understand what they mean.
- If you know that you have been silly and selfish, saying sorry will make you feel better.
- There is always plenty of love for everyone — especially when you are kind and generous.

The Wisdom
in the Puddle

Relax, be very still and listen carefully to this story about a boy called Jack. He learned something important about friendship when an angel sent him a mysterious message. Now, close your eyes and imagine you can hear rain pitter-pattering against the window. It's such a soft, peaceful sound.

On just such a rainy day, Jack was at school. It was playtime and, despite the rain, the teachers told everyone to play outside. Jack was one of the last to go – his jacket was nowhere to be seen.

"Come along, Jack, hurry up and make the most of your break!" Miss Creek said. She bustled past Jack on her way to the staff room with a big pile of exercise books in her arms. "If you don't get a move on, playtime will be over by the time you get outside!"

"Oh, where is the stupid thing?" Jack muttered aloud. Cameron and the others would already be playing soccer by now. Miss Creek had gone, letting the door shut behind her with a brisk slam. Jack wasn't expecting anyone to answer.

But someone did. "Here's your jacket. It was lying on the floor. I think it must have fallen off your hook when everyone rushed out."

Jack looked up. It was Stevie, sitting quietly on the bench, holding Jack's coat. Miss Creek obviously hadn't noticed Stevie either. He was one of those people who just seemed to fade into the background.

"Thanks." Jack took the coat, smiling to be polite. There was something about Stevie that made him feel uneasy. Maybe it was because he didn't laugh and shout like the other children. He was a bit like a shadow, always quiet, always watching.

Stevie and Jack had been in the same class for years, but this was the first time that Jack had really spoken to him. He wondered what would happen if one of his friends saw him talking to Stevie now – someone like Cameron, who liked to tease? Cameron had often said he thought Stevie was really weird. He might even start saying he thought Jack was weird, too!

"Maybe I should see if Stevie wants to play soccer with us?" Jack thought. But then he imagined Cameron laughing at him. It just wasn't worth the trouble. Anyway, it was obvious that Stevie was happiest when he was on his own. He was probably really bad at soccer, too.

Jack rushed outside into the rain, taking one last look at the thin, quiet boy who was sitting alone on the bench. Stevie was staring down at his feet now, eyes fixed on his old battered trainers.

"Hey, Jack, where have you been?" Cameron shouted from across the playground. "You're in goal. Alex is no good at it."

"Well, you try it yourself then, Cameron," Alex muttered. He trudged past Jack, leaving the goalposts free. "I'm not that bad!"

"Don't worry about him, he's just got a big mouth," Jack said to Alex, who smiled.

Jack waited in goal while his friends kicked the ball about at the far end of the pitch. He stared down at a puddle by his feet. He wondered what it would be like to be Stevie, to be always on his own. He realized that he didn't really feel like playing soccer. And anyway the game seemed to have got stuck down at the opposite goalposts. Cameron was obviously desperate to score but he wasn't passing the ball to anyone.

Jack sighed, staring down at the puddle again – and this time he got the shock of his life. There was something that looked like writing in the water. It was floating on the surface like the rainbow colours in petrol. Jack rubbed his eyes, then looked again.

Stevie has nobody, Jack read.

Jack's heart started to pound. Was he imagining this? He rubbed his eyes again and crouched down to get a closer look. As he watched the letters blurred and shifted to make new words.

Why not give him a chance? he read.

Jack barely noticed as the ball shot straight past him and into the goal. He didn't even hear the shouting from the far end of the pitch. How on earth had writing got into the puddle? What did it all mean?

When Jack looked down again, all trace of the writing had completely vanished. All he could see was his own reflection in a puddle pockmarked with raindrops, his eyes opened wide. He had the strangest feeling that someone was watching him – but when he looked up, no one was there.

Jack could hardly believe what he'd seen, but at the same time he knew he wasn't going crazy. He knew that he hadn't imagined the mysterious message and he knew what he had to do.

Jack got to his feet and started walking down the pitch in the rain. He felt a strange warmth inside, as if he'd just drunk a huge cup of hot chocolate. He ignored Cameron and Alex, who were yelling at him to stop. They could wait. Jack walked across the playground, back to where Stevie was sitting alone in the cloakroom. It was time to make friends.

Affirmations

- Angels can guide us in the most unusual ways, even by sending us strange messages when we least expect them.
- Don't be afraid to do what you believe is right, even if you are worried about what others might think. People will respect your strength of character.
- It's important to try to be friends with everyone, so that no one feels lonely or left out.

Lost in
the Wood

Relax, be very still and listen carefully to this story about a boy called Toby, who overcame his fear of heights thanks to a furry angel. Toby will tell his own story.

"My name's Toby. Well, you know that already. So, a while ago I didn't really have any friends. I'd always been a bit of a loner, you see. It's not that I didn't like the other kids. I just felt shy when they asked me to play with them.

"I lived with my mum in a village on the edge of a wood. One hot day, the other kids went to swim in the river. They asked me to come but I said I was helping my mother. In fact, I love swimming but I thought I had to play it cool and pretend I liked being on my own.

"So, that's why I was indoors on my own when Josh came past. His family had just moved in next door and he hadn't met any other kids yet, only me.

"'Why are you inside?' Josh yelled through the window. 'It's hot! Let's go exploring in the woods.'

"I almost said no but the sun was shining and being stuck indoors didn't seem like much fun.

"'OK, let's go. I know all the paths in the wood!' I said — even though I didn't.

"That day was the best fun ever. We paddled into the middle of a stream and built a dam from sticks and stones. We even saw a snake!

"By the time we set off back, the sun was starting to set. That's when everything began to go wrong. I must have taken the wrong fork in the path. Half an hour later, it was almost dark and we were still in the woods.

"'You've lived here the longest,' said Josh. 'Climb up a tree to see where we are.'

"I hated climbing trees. Truth is, I was scared stiff of heights. But I couldn't say no because Josh would think I was a coward. And it was my fault we were lost.

"Branch by branch I started to climb a tree. As I got further away from the ground my stomach started to turn over. I felt dizzy. I was sure I was going to fall!

"That's when I looked up and saw the squirrel. He was sitting on a branch staring at me. He ran along the branch, then he stopped and looked back. It was like he was asking me to follow him and showing me that

126

climbing trees was easy. I heard a voice in my head saying, 'You can do it! Be brave!'

"Before I knew it, I was up on the next branch and following the squirrel. He led me right to the top of the tree. For the first time, I wasn't frightened of heights. Best of all, I could see the roofs of the village a short way away. We weren't lost at all!

"Josh said I was the bravest guy he'd ever met and after that we were best friends. Some of the other kids became our friends, too. Pretty soon we had our own gang.

"I've never told anyone about the squirrel until now. It might sound strange – I knew he wasn't a squirrel at all, he was an angel who had come to help me. And I wanted to keep that a special secret between him and me – and you, of course."

Affirmations

◇◇◇◇◇◇◇◇◇◇◇◇◇◇◇◇◇◇

- Angels often appear to us in animal form, so keep your eyes open!
- A real friendship with just one person is worth more than having lots of friends you don't actually like that much.
- If you face your fear, you often find that things are not so scary after all.

Jack and the Snowman

Relax, be very still and listen carefully to this story about Billy, who loved adventures.

It was winter. It felt to most people as if it had been winter for ever and they were fed up. The snow was still piled up high on the ground and icicles dangled from the houses. But Billy loved winter — he loved tobogganing and he loved ice-skating. And he loved making angel wings. That's when you lie down in the snow and wave your arms up and down to make the shape of the wings. He didn't want winter to end — ever.

There was an ice rink near Billy's house. He went skating there every afternoon after school with his friends, Elsie and Joe. Billy's dog, Jed, always came too. Near the rink was a large frozen lake. Every time they passed the lake, Billy thought how much fun it would be skate on it. The ice rink was always crowded, but he wouldn't have to share the lake with anyone. He'd be free to skate as fast as he liked.

"Never skate on frozen lakes or ponds," his parents always told him. "You can never be sure how thick the ice is. It's dangerous, Billy. If the ice cracks you'll fall in." But the ice on this lake looked quite strong to Billy.

At the centre of the lake was a small island that could be reached by a footbridge. One day, as the children walked toward the ice rink, they saw that someone had built a huge snowman on the island. He had a carrot for a nose, a scarf around his neck and a scruffy hat.

"Look at that," Billy called to the others. "Look at that fantastic snowman!"

Jed started barking excitedly and ran out on to the frozen lake, heading for the snowman.

"Jed, come back!" yelled Elsie. "It's not safe." And Jed did come back, his tail between his legs.

Billy laughed at Elsie for being so silly. "The ice is strong enough for Jed. I bet it could take my weight," he said. "In fact, I bet I could skate all the way around the island."

"Don't be so stupid," Elsie said. "Haven't you noticed how much warmer it is today? The icicles on my roof were starting to melt this morning. Spring is coming! The ice will start breaking up soon. If you step on it you'll fall in."

But the more Billy was told not to do something, the more he wanted to do it. He knew better than any girl. Ignoring Elsie, he pulled on his skates ready to set out for the lake. "I'll show her who's stupid," he thought.

Just then something caught Billy's eye – a bright splash of colour in the white winter day. It was a bird, the most brilliantly coloured bird Billy had ever seen. It was red, blue and green, with long tail feathers and a great red crest on top of its head. The bird opened its beak and started to sing. It made a beautiful sound, like a bell ringing out.

The bird looked like it belonged in the steamy rainforest, not in a snowy winter world. Billy thought how strange it was to see a bird like that in the snow. And he wondered if maybe Elsie was right, if maybe the bird also knew that spring was on its way.

Billy pushed the idea from his mind. He knew what he wanted to do and nothing would prevent him. He stepped on to the ice, ready to skate off.

Then he looked down – and stopped. He could see a bright fish, swimming just beneath the ice. The fish was gold and green, and just as dazzling as the bird. It looked tropical. But that was impossible, of course. How could a tropical fish survive in a frozen lake?

Billy stared at the fish. The water couldn't be that cold, he thought, if a fish could swim in it. Could Elsie be right? Was he really being stupid? But Billy didn't like the idea that he could be wrong one little bit. He was going to skate to the snowman, come what may.

Then, as he looked across the lake, Billy saw the strangest thing yet of all the strange things that had happened that day. He could have sworn the snowman was lifting up his hat and waving at him. Billy blinked and rubbed his eyes. It looked like the snowman was shaking his head!

Now Billy could hear a voice calling to him, a weird sparkly voice that sounded like ice cubes tinkling in a glass. It seemed to be coming from the snowman himself. And it sounded like the snowman was whispering, "Don't skate, Billy. Don't skate!"

Billy looked around to Elsie and Joe. "Did you hear that?" he asked them. "Did you see that?"

"What?" said Elsie. "You mean the
sound of the snowman falling down?"

Billy saw that the snowman's head
had toppled from his body.

"Look, the snowman is melting!" said
Elsie. "It really is spring. I told you so."

Billy looked at the lake. He could see that
cracks were beginning to form all over the ice.
"So the snowman was looking out for me," he said
to himself. "And so was that amazing tropical bird and the
fish, too! I guess I'm really lucky. Skating would have been
very dangerous."

"Come on," called Joe. "Let's make some angel wings
while there's still some snow to do it."

Affirmations

- Angels are all around us, wanting us to do the right thing and giving us little
  signs that we may not notice.
- Our friends help us to understand the world. It's good to consider other
  people's opinions before we make up our own mind.
- Sometimes nature can be dangerous as well as beautiful. In that case, you can
  always enjoy it at a distance, from a safe place such as a footpath.

Taking the Stories Further

Visualization means conjuring up pictures in your mind at will. We all know what it's like to imagine a scene, but we can't necessarily control what we imagine – even as adults we spend too much time thinking about things that *might* happen. Children are natural visualizers but usually have a habit of flitting from one thought to another, rather than settling to explore a single imaginary scene.

Controlled visualization is a wonderful skill. A child who can create and control characters and settings in his mind gains in self-confidence and empathy, as well as in the practical skills of concentration and creativity. Later, as he starts to face situations that require courage and calmness, you can encourage him to use visualization to, for example, picture himself doing well in an exam or playing brilliantly in a music recital. It is well known that the athletes who spend time before a race imagining themselves crossing the finishing line have the edge over their competitors.

Like all skills, visualization is easier and more effective the more we practise it. Many children enjoy visualization games. Try showing your child an unusual object and then asking him to close his eyes and describe it in as much detail as possible. Or you could ask him to picture something he knows very well, for example a favourite toy. Later, he can try something more imaginative, such as describing a journey along a river to the sea.

You can also use the stories in this book to encourage your child to visualize – and really bring the tales alive for him. Remember that visualization doesn't just have to be about seeing: he can imagine smells, sounds, feelings and tastes, too. However, the illustrations that accompany each story are a good place to start. There are also some short exercises on the following pages, to help you both to get the hang of it.

As a child approaches the border between wakefulness and sleep, he enters a magical terrain where the mind relaxes and imagination takes control. This is the perfect time for visualizations and other imaginative adventures, which is why this collection is meant to be shared at bedtime. But once your child has the power to visualize at will, he will be able to use his imaginative thinking whenever and wherever he wants.

A First Visualization

Successful visualization requires both relaxation and concentration – both of which are often in short supply when it comes to children. This step-by-step guide is designed to help you to lead your child along the path of a first creative visualization.

Before you start, ask your child if she'd like to try visualizing one of the angels in the book with you. Tell her that it's easiest to see an imaginary picture when our minds are clear of other thoughts, but that she should not worry if she gets distracted. She can simply tell the thought she'll come back to it later and put it to one side.

Step 1 Ask your child to sit up in a comfortable position with her eyes closed. Ask her to breathe in and out a few times, and as she does so to think about the breath travelling in through her nose and out through her mouth. Try breathing aloud along with her, to help her to keep a steady rhythm.

Step 2 When she seems calm, ask her to imagine a white light behind her eyes. Tell her that this is a magic light that will allow her to see anything that she wants to see.

Step 3 As she focuses on the light, ask your child to imagine an angel. She may want a traditional angel with wings or perhaps one of the angels that appear in an unusual form, such as the stag in "The Perfect Picture". Help her by describing the angel's appearance. For example: "His huge antlers spread above him like wings. In the setting sun, he looks as if he's made from gold."

Step 4 Now describe what the angel does. You might say, "When the stag raises his head from the stream, he stares straight at the boy who is watching him. It's as if he knows the boy is there and wants him to have the chance of a photograph, after all the hours of waiting."

Step 5 Now say something like: "The stag has disappeared. The sun has set and it's quiet in the wood. Let the light in your mind fade away, and with it the picture of the stag. Feel the happiness and peace that the angel has left behind."

What's in the Clouds?

Children are kept so busy these days that it's good to encourage them to spend some time "doing nothing". When your child's mind is open and relaxed he will start to really notice everyday things such as the clouds in the sky — and begin to weave stories around them.

"Imagine it's a summer's day and you are lying on your back staring up at the sky. The grass is pricking your arms and you can hear birdsong and smell a tree in flower close by. You are watching clouds move slowly across the sky, changing shape. What can you see? The clouds are white and fluffy, like lambs in a field. One of them is bigger than the others. That's the mother, nudging her lambs home. Now the clouds are piling together in a mound that looks just like a giant ice cream. Now what can you see? The clouds are dissolving and there's only one big cloud left that looks a little bit like an angel. You can make out wings and a trailing robe. There's a golden glow around her head. Suddenly the sun breaks through. When you look back the angel has gone and the clouds have dissolved into the blue sky."

The Secret Tower

Children love the idea of a place that belongs to them alone. Your child will probably have her own ideas about her special place, but here are a few to get you started:

"Imagine that you have a magical power: you can fly! You can fly above people's heads, tickling their hair. You can swoop over the rooftops and peep through the windows. And when you want to be on your own, you can fly up into the air, as high as the birds. There's a mountain with thick forest and steep cliffs on all sides. No one can climb it, but you are flying up, the wind supporting your legs and arms as you wave to the birds nesting in the cliffs, and turn somersaults in the air. Now the city is like a toy town far below. At the very top of the mountain is a stone tower. Only you have a key. You let yourself in, climb a spiral staircase and find a cosy room with a soft bed and lots of good things to eat and drink, and your favourite toys and books. There's a window seat where you can look out over the sea, the hills, all the towns. You can stay in your tower as long as you want, and when you are ready to come back, all you have to do is fly down."

Meet Your Special Angel

The idea of an angel just for him can help a child to feel extra-special, give him confidence and be a source of comfort. If your child asks you about his guardian angel, try this visualization to help him to discover more for himself.

"Imagine a white light behind your eyes. This is the spotlight into which your guardian angel will step. Tell your angel that you would very much like to meet her and ask if she would show herself to you. Now wait … what do you see? Maybe your angel doesn't look the way you expect. Perhaps you can see an animal or something else altogether. If your angel is smiling at you, smile back: it's only polite! Say hello to her and thank her for showing herself to you. Now listen. Can you hear her voice? If you are lucky, she may speak to you as well. See how your angel looks at you with such tenderness. She is telling you that you must never feel lonely, because she is always looking after you. Now it is time to say goodbye. She is fading, the light is dissolving into thousands of tiny stars. She is gone, and you feel as if you are wrapped in a warm cloud of love and happiness."

Index of Values and Issues

These two complementary indexes cover the specific topics that the twenty-two stories of this book are designed to address directly or by implication. The same topics are covered from two different perspectives: positive (Values) and negative (Issues). Each index reference consists of an abbreviated story title, followed by the page number on which the story begins.

Acknowledgments

The Publishers would like to thank the four storytellers for writing the tales listed below:

Anne Civardi
"The Heroine of the Crow's Nest"

Lou Kuenzler
"Dad's Big Day", "The Little Wooden Box", "On the Ropes", "The Perfect Picture", "The Smallest Giant"

Katy Jane Moran
"Lily's School Play", "The Magic Trick", "The Mysterious Cowboy", "Odd One Out", "The Wisdom in the Puddle"

Karen Wallace
"The Flying Horse", "Grandad's Pumpkin", "The Honest Shepherd", "The Kind Monkey", "Light in the Dark", "Lost in the Wood", "The Nesting Swallows", "The Old Man and the Seesaw", "The Proud Prince", "The Turquoise Bird"